nickelodeon™

THE CLEAN, GREEN RESCUE!

By Cara Stevens • Illustrated by Heather Martinez

Random House 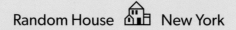 New York

rhcbooks.com

ISBN 978-0-593-30992-6 (trade)

Printed in the United States of America

10 9 8 7 6 5 4 3 2 1

It was a sunny day in Adventure Bay, and the PAW Patrol was busy fixing up Main Street Park. They were planting flowers and trees and picking up litter.

"Great work, team," said Ryder. "The park is going to look great for tomorrow's We Love the Earth Fun Fair!"

"The birds seem to like the new trees we planted," Skye announced as she zoomed overhead.

"And these new flowers smell really pretty," Rubble declared.

Chase took a sniff and let out a big sneeze. *"ACHOO!"*

"Everything is going to be perfect for the fair," Ryder said.
"And the concert," Marshall added. "I can't believe Luke Stars is doing a show here tomorrow!"

"I'm going to dance, dance, DANCE!" said Rubble.
"Then we'd better head back to the Lookout and get some sleep," said Ryder.

That night, a big storm hit Adventure Bay. Wind howled, rain poured, and thunder rolled. All the noise woke Rubble and Chase, so they got up and looked out a window.

"Will this ruin the fair?" Rubble asked.

"I hope not," Chase replied. "I'm sure it will end by morning."

Chase was right. By morning, the rain had stopped and the sun was shining. But the storm had done some damage. Ryder got an emergency call on his PupPad.

It was Farmer Al. "Lightning struck our big oak tree last night," he said. "It fell across the road. We won't be able to get to the fair tonight."

"Don't worry, Farmer Al," said Ryder. "The PAW Patrol is on the roll!"

Ryder called the team to the Lookout.

Rubble was dancing with excitement. "Do you want us to get ready for the concert?" he asked.

"Not yet," Ryder answered. "Farmer Al needs help cleaning up after the storm."

Ryder passed out the assignments.

"Chase," he said, "I'll need you and Marshall to head to the farm to take a big fallen oak tree off the road."

"I'm fired up!" Marshall said.

He and Chase ran to their trucks and raced to help.

At the farm, Farmer Yumi and Farmer Al were waiting for Chase and Marshall by the fallen tree. When the pups arrived, the tree seemed even bigger to them than Ryder had said.

"How did this oak tree get so big?" Marshall asked.

"It was two hundred years old," Farmer Yumi told them. "Squirrels, deer, and other animals ate the acorns that fell from its branches. Birds, bugs, and animals lived inside the tree, too. It helped clean our air, and it gave us shade."

Chase used his winch to pull the tree off the road.
"We can plant new trees, like we did at the park," Marshall suggested
He helped Farmer Yumi plant a few smaller trees nearby.
"These trees grow quickly," Farmer Yumi said. "They'll be big and
strong soon."

Chase helped load the wood from the fallen tree into Farmer Al's truck. "There must be something we can make from all this great wood." "Right," Farmer Al agreed. "We can't waste it." He thought for a moment. "I have an idea—it will be a surprise!"

Meanwhile, back at the Lookout, Ryder got a call from Cap'n Turbot. "Litter, the Ryder is covered in beach," said Cap'n Turbot. "I mean . . . Ryder, the beach is covered in litter from the storm."

"We're on it!" Ryder replied, then turned to the pups.

"Rocky, bring your recycling truck to the beach," he said. "We need to pick up all the trash that landed there from the storm."

"If there's trash on the beach, it's probably in the water, too," Zuma replied. "I can help!"

"That's a great idea!" said Ryder. "In fact, maybe we should all go and pitch in."

Just then, Chase called Ryder on his PupPad. "Marshall and I have cleaned up the farm, Ryder, sir. What else can we do to help?"

"Great job, pups," Ryder said. "Join us on the beach. We have to clean up there, too."

"We're on the case!" Chase exclaimed.

Chase and Marshall rolled up to the beach, ready to help their friends
"There's a lot of trash here," Chase said.
"There sure is," Zuma said. He held up a plastic bag. "The wind blows
bags like these all over Adventure Bay. Lots of them end up in the ocean."

"Sometimes turtles and seals think the floating bags are food," Rocky added.

"Then we'd better clean this up right away!" said Chase.

Cap'n Turbot and the pups got to work. Rocky set up recycling stations and showed his friends how to sort the litter.

"Marshall," said Rocky, "can you stack the cardboard and paper? Chase, pick up all the plastic you can find. Don't touch anything that looks sharp or dangerous."

Zuma set out in his hovercraft. He threw a net into the water and dragged it behind the boat to collect the litter.

Zuma returned to shore, his net filled with litter. The pups recognized things in the net that they used every day, like straws, plastic soda can rings, water bottles, and snack bags.

"Seabirds and fish could get tangled in trash that ends up in the water," Rocky said. "We should recycle all this plastic and keep it out of our water for good."

With everyone working together, the last of the litter was picked up and sorted.

"Great work, pups," said Ryder.

"Positively perfect," Cap'n Turbot agreed. "This big beach is beautiful again!"

"And just in time," said Chase. "The fair is about to start."
"And the concert!" Rubble added excitedly.
Then Ryder received another call.

It was Luke Stars!

"There was a mudslide on Mountain Road!" he reported. "My tour bus is stuck. I don't know if I'm going to make it to the fair."

"Don't worry," Ryder replied. "We'll be right there!"

The PAW Patrol rolled to the rescue.

Ryder and the team found the tour bus. It was surrounded by mud and blocked by giant boulders that had rolled down the mountain.

Luke leaned out the window and waved to the pups. "I'm so glad you're here! Do you think you can help?"

"Don't worry," Rubble called. "We'll have you out in no time." He turned to Ryder. "What should we do?"

"Rubble, I need you to use your Digger to shovel the mud out of the way and lift those rocks," said Ryder.

"I can dig it!" Rubble exclaimed.

Ryder turned to Chase. "And I need your winch to pull out some of the bigger boulders."

"I'm on it!" Chase replied.

While the pups worked, Rocky asked Ryder how such a big mudslide could have happened.

"The weather is warmer this year," said Ryder. "The snow melted quickly and loosened the dirt that held the rocks. The storm washed everything down the hill."

"There's a lot of mud, and we're moving slowly," Rubble reported to Ryder. "I don't know if we can get the bus out in time for the concert!"

"Marshall, can you use your water cannons to help clear away the mud?" Ryder asked. "And, Skye, can you give Luke a lift to the show?" The two pups answered yes, then sprang into action.

Meanwhile, at Main Street Park, the fair was all set up.
But Mayor Goodway was getting nervous.

"We have games and face painting," she said.
"Everything we need for a fun day. All we're missing
is our main attraction. Where could Luke Stars be,
Chickaletta?"

WE ♥ OUR PARK

Just then, Skye zoomed over the crowd in her helicopter, carrying Luke Stars in a rescue harness. She set him gently on the stage, and everyone cheered!

"The PAW Patrol sure knows how to make an entrance!" the mayor exclaimed.

Just as Luke started his first song, the PAW Patrol arrived at the park with the tour bus. It was completely clean and looking good as new. They ran to the show and found Farmer Yumi and Farmer Al, who unveiled their surprise.

"We made this picnic table from the tree that fell at the farm," said Farmer Al. "Now whenever anyone comes to this wonderful park, they'll remember how important it is not to waste anything."

"That's a great idea!" Ryder exclaimed.

"Don't lose it—reuse it!" said Rocky.

Luke Stars called Ryder and the pups onto the stage with him.
"This next song," he told the crowd, "is dedicated to the PAW Patrol.
Without them, today would not have happened. They made this park
beautiful, and they got me here on time!"

"Don't mention it," Ryder said. "We love our town, and we like to keep it clean and help our friends. It's fun—and not hard to do when we all work together."

"It's almost as fun as dancing!" giggled Rubble.

As the sun set, the music started to play. Luke began singing, and everyone danced. It was the perfect end to a very busy day.